The Jesus Year

To my parents, Peter and Kaliopi.

Contents

A Guide to Decorating	9
The Evaluators	27
Familia	49
The Jesus Year	77
A Raising	87
Hasard	99
Going to Market	131
Acknowledgements	143

A Guide to Decorating

Sheila's mother jaundiced the year she spent dying, even the whites of her eyes. Her black hair greyed and then, except for downy tufts at her temples, fell out.

The first day in the home, she sat in her new bed, an adjustable single with bars on the side, her skinny legs spread so that her feet rested on the metal. Wires connected the bed to a panel of beeping instruments.

"Look, honey, I'm pregnant." Maureen smoothed the worn strawberry print of her nightgown across and under her distended belly, grinned. Her teeth had been yellow a long time already.

"Remember, you have to water this one every

week," Sheila said, placing the spider plant on the bedside table.

"Move it there." Maureen pointed to the windowsill, through which the other brown brick wing of the unit was visible.

"It doesn't need light, Mom," Sheila said.

"I don't want to knock it."

Sheila had salvaged the plant, the tips of its leaves brown, from her mother's house. She had searched the usual spots: between the mattress, inside the toilet tank, behind bacon and ice cubes in the freezer. They collected two dozen bottles, some almost empty, but most full.

The basement was packed to the ceiling and five boxes deep.

"It doesn't stink," Hank had said. He took three boxes at a time because of his gangly arms.

"She always rinses them with soap and lets them dry." Sheila could hoist only two boxes, with effort.

They made $473 from the bottles, and another $550 from the garage sale. It had started to rain midday and they moved the sale inside, selling the dusty rose velour couch and a tube TV, a VCR, and all the china that matched nothing. Sheila salvaged her father's tool belt and her collection of junior high and high school track medals.

Sheila and Hank took possession of the condo a month after Maureen's house sold. Sheila pushed the wheelchair right up to the bay window that faced east. They were on the third floor. The bluff's spring grass, still brown, was turning a reflected pink.

"What do you think?" Hank asked. Maureen had a couple hours before they returned to the hospice.

"It has good light," Maureen said. She had started wearing dark tinted glasses for her eyes. The previous owners had painted the walls a serious taupe that, in shadow, turned brown.

They ordered a thin-crust prosciutto, basil, and mozzarella pizza from the next block over.

"Smells yummy!" Maureen said, sucking back her Sprite. She nibbled on Sheila's abandoned crust. Sheila sat on the upturned milk crate she brought the cleaning supplies in, and Hank kneeled on his jacket.

The floor where the previous owners had placed their kitchen table was mottled with sticky splatters, the wood resin dulled. Maureen fell asleep in the wheelchair while Sheila scrubbed the floor with baking soda. After Hank drove Maureen to the Home, Sheila cracked a bottle of pale ale and ate the last piece of pizza, the pork cold and salty.

Hank cradled the paint chip in his palm like a melting chocolate.

"Eggshell isn't accurate. Whose egg? Brown chickens lay brown eggs, blue birds lay blue eggs," Sheila said. She spun a colour wheel, a whirl of infant pastels.

The paint spinner chugged with another couple's choice. The couple shared shaved heads and had walked in after Sheila and Hank. They were already paying.

"This eggshell clearly belongs to a white bird." Now Hank held the chip like a cigarette between his index and third fingers.

"I don't want racist paint."

"What's wrong with you?" He bent the chip in half with his thumb.

"Okay, I don't want boring-ass paint."

"Lance said classic neutrals sell." Lance was Hank's cousin, their real estate agent.

"That's because most people want something nice and easy to paint over. Christ."

The shaved couple had chosen tangerine and lime green from a non-toxic paint catalogue, and Sheila reached for it across the scuffed chrome table.

"Yellow, look."

"Dear God."

The paint mixer shook their shade of sun, which, when Sheila opened it at home, was the colour of blooming rapeseed, or mustard.

The marathon began right outside their window: pumping techno and a loop of "Eye of the Tiger." Sheila and Hank sipped coffee. The night before had ended only hours earlier, the two bottles of Malbec and the stained wine glasses empty on the faded wood of the patio table. The lead-up to the race took two hours, the participants crowding into a holding pen, arranged by expected end time.

The little blond boy across the street danced, kicking his heels to his bottom and then shaking his hips. His parents watched him and drank out of mugs and laughed with open mouths. When the starter pistol cracked, the boy startled and began to cry. The commotion of runners, all ten thousand of them shuffling forward, their wrists and calves covered in throwaway strips of cotton, distracted him. He ran back and forth, zooming in the street, the area blocked to traffic. The heaviest runners pooled at the back, a 5:35 sign hoisted above them, buttocks and bosoms squeezed tightly into Lycra.

The runners littered the street with disposable arm and leg warmers, water bottles. The marathon passed by the Home, and this is what Sheila would have talked to her mother about that afternoon, but Maureen had lost consciousness. Underneath eyelids, her dim eyes switched back and forth. She smelled of raw meat, and Sheila began the wait.

Sheila had not needed to wait long for her father's death. It came quick and angry, bursting tumours in his abdomen that had kept him from eating citrus or spice for the last ten years of his life. He drank a carton of 2% milk nightly and lay on the couch, rubbing his belly with one hand while belching softly into the other.

The night before the wedding, he had visited Sheila in the childhood bedroom she hadn't occupied since high school, four years earlier. The oxygen machine beeped from down the hall. He sat on the bed and said, "You're not doing this for me?"

They had practiced going down the aisle only once in the backyard, and her mother had said,

"Sheila, don't get your veil caught on that walker tomorrow."

"We love each other," Sheila said. She was writing the words she'd say to Hank the next day, after the vows and before the I Dos.

"This you need to look at, after the wedding." He handed her a sealed manila envelope.

She wrote, "I have never loved anyone so much," and read the words to Hank the next day in the park a block from her parents' house.

The night of their wedding, they held a barbeque for the dozen guests. Uncle Robin, her father's brother, manned the grill and bar. As Aunt Laurie wheeled out the wedding cake, Sheila's mother started to sway like she was dancing, her long red skirt swinging before the first rib eye was served.

Uncle Robin grabbed Maureen's forearm as she stumbled close to the grill, and she poured the drink, clear vodka with ice cubes shaped like daisies, onto the coals. The hot steam burned her arm a bright pink, and Uncle Robin took her to the emergency, wearing the Eat Up or Shut Up apron Sheila had bought her dad for Father's Day when she was fourteen. It was stained across the front, pink smears that bleach would not remove.

Sheila's cousin Adelle ordered fried chicken

and Chinese food, chicken balls, chow mein, and scrawny broccolini with beef. They ate off paper plates and drank red wine from the goblets Uncle Robin and Aunt Laurie had given them.

Sheila met with the lawyer the day after the marathon and signed originals of the papers her father had drawn up for her six years earlier. She would go to the bank the next day.

"I'd like to visit the cottage next weekend," Sheila said. She was arranging orange gerbers in a pale green vase. She cut the stems with a steak knife.

"Next week? That's soon." Hank had made breakfast, and the extra hash browns were cold in the pan. Sheila popped one in her mouth.

"These are too spicy," she said.

They waited for three hours on the way to Sicamous; the single lane highway over the mountains was blocked both ways because of the wreck.

"I have to pee," Sheila sang the ees like in a

pop song, "ee ee ee."

Three helicopters swinging gurneys arrived overhead, and Sheila and Hank could not speak for the noise.

The truck behind them, two young men in board shorts and two blondes in sun dresses, turned up their stereo, Eminem, and drank beer out of cans while sitting in the box.

Once the line of cars started, the young people tossed their cans in the ditch. Sheila and Hank reached a gas station only five kilometres away.

Sheila had brought three different colour palettes for the cabin.

"Red and grey? A pop and a neutral." She held the chips up to the forest-green walls.

"All the curtains have to go." Sheila gestured to the country plaid, green and blue, a frilled work shirt.

"It's up to you," Hank said, sipping a beer.

They brought Maureen a gift at Christmas, grapefruit-scented hand lotion. Sheila tugged her mother's rings off and massaged the hands, plump from bloating.

The IV inserted at the left wrist, and Sheila avoided the brown bruised skin.

She finished massaging and slid the wedding ring, a gold sliver of a band with three diamonds buttressed off it, and the sapphire solitaire Maureen wore on her right index finger, back on the fingers. They both stuck at the knuckles, and even with the application of more lotion, would not slide past the bulging knots of bone.

Sheila slipped the rings into the zippered change pocket of her wallet.

"Does she know we're here?" Hank asked. Maureen's lips had parted.

"She can't feel a thing."

Sheila received the call in the spring. Lynn, an interior designer, was reviewing photos of the cabin. The cabin had stayed empty all winter because of the roads, but Sheila and Hank planned on hosting a weekend getaway party in July.

"I think coral paint would work well here," Lynn said, pointing to a photo of the kitchen. Sheila had spread the colour wheels and fabric swatches across the glass kitchen table.

Sheila had decorated the condo herself, adding turquoise trim to the walls and buying a red leather couch that spanned the length of the living room wall and sat low on thin grey columns. An original print, grey and blue swirls, an abstract storm, hung above the couch. When Lynn walked into the condo, her briefcase and sample case in hand, she scanned the room and nodded. "Nice mix of urban and rough chic," she had said.

Lynn would stay and draft some sample boards. Sheila said she would only be a minute.

"Her vitals have been changing, some fluctuations. We thought you should know," Nurse Janine said, patting Maureen's hand. She left the room, and Sheila took last week's tulips to the bathroom, threw them into the garbage can, and rinsed the vase in the bathtub. On the toilet seat, five inches of tan plastic, rested a drop of urine. She put the new flowers, purple lilies, in the vase and filled it with lukewarm water.

Maureen was staring straight up at the ceiling, and when Sheila bent over her, she shifted her gaze. Her swollen blue-black pupils floated in the brown orbs of her irises. Maureen started blinking and then darting her eyes back and forth.

Sheila placed the vase on the bedside table, and pressed her left palm against her mother's mouth. She shielded her mother's eyes, and the eyelashes fluttered against her palm.

"Shhh," she said. "Shhh."

Sheila pinched her mother's nose and pressed the heel of her palm against Maureen's mouth more firmly. The ceiling was speckled with black dots that looked like flies. The flesh on Maureen's face had melted, skin sinking into bone, and the belly bloated and filled the space between the bars.

The eyes had frozen, and Sheila released her hands. The machine beeped steadily, and Sheila brushed her mother's eyelids closed.

Hank twisted his ankle at the lake, stumbling off the second last step to the deck. The ankle purpled and swelled.

"You have cankle!" Sheila said. She carried the bottles of wine while Adelle carried the glasses. At the funeral, Adelle and Berdecht said they'd come to the cabin; they were the only couple able to spend the weekend.

Hank sat on the deck and soaked the ankle in the lake and sucked back the wine. They slapped mosquitos, and Sheila lit a tiki torch and sprayed them down with Off. When the sun set, it was already late evening, and Hank tried to walk back to the house but screamed when he stood. He wrapped his arms around Adelle and Berdecht and hopped up the steps and across the lawn. Sheila collected the empties and the glasses, the little flags Adelle had picked up at the gas station. "To celebrate Canada Day," she had said.

Sheila had given them a tour.

"Here was a horrible lumberjack curtain, and the paint was almost Bavarian," she said, gesturing to the steel-grey kitchen wall with rust-red trim. The contractors had ripped down the drywall to reveal aged brick along one of the living room walls. Sheila had found a black wood-burning stove and tucked it into the corner next to the oak bookshelves.

"It's functional, now," she said.

"It's bloody stunning," Adelle said.

"Next year we'll do the exterior."

On the way back to the city, Hank propped his foot on the dashboard, icing the ankle with frozen peas. When they entered city limits, Sheila told him to place it on the floor.

Three police cruisers blocked their intersection, and they could not turn into their street.

They had stopped for breakfast at the diner close to the cabin early that morning. The buttered rye toast, scrambled eggs, and back bacon sat heavy in Sheila's stomach, and her lips were stained purple from the wine.

"You ask," she said.

Hank lowered his window, and an officer approached, stopped a few feet from the vehicle.

"A hit and run," the officer said. "A little boy."

A dog growled from one of the cruisers, then barked, invisible behind black glass.

"Is he okay?" Hank asked.

"No telling. Ma'am, you'll have to park on the street."

They drove to Zarillo's a block away and ordered two thin-crust pizzas and a pint each.

"That poor family," Hank said, mopping up spilt beer with a paper napkin.

"You'd think they'd catch the guy," Sheila said. The bubbles from the beer were settling her stomach.

"Maybe they already have," Hank said. "My ankle feels better."

They ordered a second and then a third round, and the street was clear by the time they finished.

Around midnight, a police car pulled up to the house across the street. An officer escorted the parents to the door, shaking the father's hand and patting the mother on the back. When the officer turned, the woman brought her palms to her face, and her husband wrapped his arms around her.

Sheila went back to the bedroom. She slid underneath the covers, warm and pungent with Hank's heat and the odour of beer. She spooned him and slipped her hand beneath the elastic band of his shorts.

"Come here," she whispered, and nudged Hank awake.

The Evaluators

Everyone said Tofino was just a dream.

"The ends of the earth," Martha, Olivia's department head, had said. "We saw whales breach during dinner once."

It was Henry's idea to come here. They walked separately, Henry first, down the long staircase through the rainforest to the beach. Olivia waited her turn and then gripped the railing the whole way. Her sweating feet slid forward and strained the thin white leather straps of her sandals. She breathed hard through the thick air.

She took the sandals off at the bottom of the stairs because of the sand and scooped them up in one hand. In the other, she carried her bouquet, three pink peonies wrapped together with ribbon, ordered from a local florist who operated out of a garage. The wind off the water dried the sweat on Olivia's face.

Across the beach, Henry stood with the white-bearded JP. He wore tan full-length pants and a white long-sleeved button-down. The JP and the male witness were in board shorts and Hawaiian shirts, orange and yellow flowers bright against the grey sky and silver water. The other witness, in a mauve cocktail dress split up the thigh with a ruffled hem, snapped pictures of Olivia baring teeth in a smile as she walked towards Henry. Closer to the waves, Olivia set her shoes down to hold her skirt, which was chiffon and flying up with every gust off the ocean. She tasted salt on her upper lip.

"We're gathered here today," the JP started.

Henry grinned. A flake of skin, the size of a sesame seed, rested on his shaved chin. Surfers bobbed on their boards, slick seals, everyone wearing black neoprene wetsuits. Henry had said there would be surfing, but Olivia hadn't pictured the suits.

When it came time to exchange the rings, Olivia placed her peonies on the sand, the woman made no move to claim them, and the rose she had tucked behind her ear fell.

"I do," she said, and then Henry said, "I do." They were shouting at each other, the waves were so loud.

They signed the documents against their thighs; no one had thought to bring a clipboard.

"I pronounce you man and wife," the JP said, and they kissed, clicking teeth. The witnesses wandered off straight away, and the JP grasped Olivia's biceps and kissed her on the cheeks, clapped Henry on the back.

"Good luck," he said. "Maybe I'll see you on the surf."

When he'd gone, Olivia said, "Why would he say man and wife?"

She bent down to pick up the rose and the bouquet. A red crab like a benign spider crawled in and out of the petals.

"Will it bite me?"

"Just flick it," Henry said. "Here."

"It's so cold," she said. They collected her shoes and walked back up the staircase, growing warmer with the effort and because it only blew by the water.

Bob, the owner of the Inn on the Cove, had spread red and pink petals across the sand-coloured duvet.

"Did you request this?"

"I guess it's free with the licence. Come here, wife." Henry slipped his hands up her dress and ran a finger under her garter belt.

"It's so itchy. Scratch. Yes, there. Harder."

He knelt in front of her and nibbled on her thigh.

"Why would he say *man* and wife. That's medieval."

Henry pulled back and sat on his haunches.

"I'm going to use it in class, as an example. Did you specify language to him?"

Henry stood and walked to his suitcase, rummaged and pulled out a bottle of red wine, disappeared out the door.

"Hey!" Olivia scratched at her thigh.

When Bob had showed them their room, the Driftwood Suite, the day before, he had pointed out the bed.

"I found all the wood in that cove," he said. The room and deck overlooked the ocean and the scraggly half-moon of beach where the ocean met the inn's property.

"I made it myself," he said.

"Is that legal?" Olivia had asked. He had nailed pieces of greyed driftwood to the slats of a queen canopy bed and to the bathroom doorframe. Two white bathrobes hung from the curled fingers near the ceiling.

"What drifts onto your corner of the beach is yours," Bob had said, pulling shoulder blades together. He showed Henry how to work the hot tub. Someone had glued shells and starfish to plain white picture frames. Inside the frames were photographs of the cove.

"They have everything out there," Henry said, returning. He held a corkscrew in his hand.

"Doesn't that just look like a little person?" Olivia said.

They ate their wedding dinner at a bistro. Olivia wore a navy bolero jacket over her dress; no one asked if they were newlyweds.

"Are there many bears here?" Olivia asked the server. The restaurant was called the White Bear Bistro.

"I'm from Whistler," the server said, and shrugged, setting the appetizers on the table.

Slices of translucent beef carpaccio fanned

out around a small tub of horseradish aioli.

"It looks like a flower," Olivia said, spearing and dipping a piece.

Henry had ordered oysters.

"You use the fork like this." He untethered the flesh from the shell with a tiny fork and spooned sauce before slurping it all back.

"Let it settle in your mouth," he said. "But don't chew."

She dipped her head back and spilled the sauce and brine down her chin and neck.

"Did you chew?"

"It's spicy." Olivia dabbed at her throat and cleavage, which plumped over the sweetheart bodice of her dress.

"It's an aphrodisiac," he said.

Her tongue began to thicken.

"Your skin is blotchy," Henry said.

It felt alien: hot and buzzy.

She stuck out her tongue.

Henry stood and upset the champagne, which poured into Olivia's lap.

The restaurant had an EpiPen, and the chef shot it into her thigh.

At the hospital, a squat building half a kilometre from their inn, she told the doctor she'd never had an oyster before.

"But I eat shellfish. I love lobster."

"Sometimes we develop sensitivities later on in life," he said.

"But this is an allergy?"

"Yes," he said.

Olivia already had the dress when Henry proposed. She'd bought it for a garden party. One of the other professors, an avid gardener, threw herself a birthday party in her backyard every year and invited everyone in the department. Only half, sometimes a third, came, because of vacations.

"I'll be able to attend for sure," Olivia had told Emily. When they settled on a date—it had to be after summer marks were in and before September classes began—she wrote Emily a note of apology but didn't say why she couldn't attend.

He asked her while she marked papers on his deck. He was cleaning mud out of his bicycle's gear wheel, cracking the dirt with a screwdriver.

She drank iced tea, and the glass was sweating from the heat. She set the glass on the papers because they kept blowing away. The first page of each essay had a wet patch that dried and then wrinkled.

"How's 'Feminine rhetoric is a necessary component' a thesis statement?" She drew a neat X next to the underlined sentence and wrote: "This is not a <u>thesis</u> statement, this is a vague observation." She crossed out the word *feminine* and wrote "FEMINIST."

"We spent three classes on this," she said. "They developed their own theses and evaluated each other."

On their first date eight months earlier, he had asked about her research.

"I look at nineteenth-century advertisements for domestic products and the way they depict women," she said. "And how advertising led to the rise of the housewife."

"My mother was a housewife," he said.

"She wouldn't have been if soap makers hadn't wanted her to be."

They were sipping Syrah and eating warm olives. They had started the date in late afternoon, but the café was a versatile space that transitioned into a wine bar at night. The circular yellow lamps hanging above each table dimmed. Henry's entire face was freckled; in the shadowed light he looked tanned.

"I plan the city," he said. A scar like an incision marked the skin between his thumb and forefinger. She took his hand and pressed the scar.

"A dog bit it," he said. "A giant poodle. When I was a kid. Squeeze as hard as you want, but I can't feel a thing."

She did, and her thumbnail indented the skin.

"Okay, there, that's the muscle." He removed her hand.

"I mostly reject development bids," he said.

She picked an olive out from the bowl and placed it in her mouth.

"I mostly mark papers," she said, and chewed. "They're putting up apartment buildings in my neighbourhood, where that hospital used to be."

"That was my project," he said. "You live in a trendy neighbourhood."

She rolled the pit in her mouth with her tongue.

"We both evaluate merit," she said.

"To the evaluators," Henry said, raising his glass.

No one had heard of Mayland Heights, but when she Googled his address, she saw it was just up and over the highway, wedged between car lots and low-lying industrial buildings. On their second date, she brought a raisin loaf for dessert, the only thing she could bake.

Henry barbequed prawns and served them over radicchio and iceberg. He had made the dressing himself, fresh dill and white wine vinegar.

"There's a store that only sells olive oil," she said over dinner. "They do tastings."

The house had no backyard, just a deck and a view of the mountains and downtown.

"This is the best view of the city," he said, but it overlooked the seventies bungalows and squat manufacturing trailers that littered the hill between the balcony and downtown.

"It's inner city," he said.

"What's its walkability rating?"

He bit into the body of a prawn and pulled its tail off.

"The train is just over there," he said. "By the old water tower."

"If the hill weren't there, you could see my building," she said. "Just straight ahead."

Later, when he sliced the loaf, he said, "I

thought this was chocolate." He had served them coffee in little cups, and he sipped his. "It's very moist."

She'd found the dress in a boutique she never shopped at. The clothes in the window always seemed too slinky. But the dress's chiffon skirt, which hung limply on the skinny mannequin, was infused with movement: it looked like it could spin.

"It was made for you," the woman in the shop said. Her hair was cut angled against her neck in a severe bob.

It was twice as much as she wanted to pay but, she thought, an investment.

A spray of dirt landed on the table as she marked, a chunk sinking to the bottom of her iced tea.

"Shit balls," she said. He had torn up grass with his tires in the mud; a blade stuck in the chunk in the glass.

They usually stayed at her place, but he had to clean his bike, and it was too hot for her to stay inside.

He had fallen with the bike, got it stuck in the

mud, an angry red rash peeked out of the white undershirt he wore. His hair had lightened over the summer, blondish streaks in the strawberry hue.

"We could live together," he said. "Be a team."

She'd looked up their sign match after their first date. He was a Capricorn and she a Taurus.

"You can accomplish a lot together," the sun-signs.com website read. "Capricorn is a good organizer and strategist, and Taurus will follow through with any joint plan."

"You want to move in together?"

"I want to marry you."

The dirt in the glass had melted to mud, the grass a type of garnish now.

"Yes," she said. "I will marry you."

They had planned to go surfing but Olivia still felt fragile.

"I'll walk the beach," she said. He suited up in a rental and wore a pink T-shirt like all the students; the surf school was run by women, and the shirt was its signature.

"So we don't lose you in the water," one of

the teachers said.

They parked near the beach, a different one from the ceremony. The lot was spotted with mud pits.

The teacher had tried to reassure her: "You're attached to a large flotation device," she said. "And we're all really good swimmers."

Olivia's tongue had shrunk back to size, but she felt like it could swell up again if she even touched the ocean.

She photographed the water, walked to an outcrop of rocks that was actually private property and blocked off with wire. She retreated down the shore. With her toe she wrote O ♥ H and took a picture. Her feet sank in the wetter sand. Little bubbles rose up, breaking the surface, sand creatures trying to breathe.

When she got back to their spot, Henry and the rest of them were in the water. No one was catching a wave.

A woman in her forties ran back ashore, pulling the board by her ankle. Her wetsuit hugged the curve of her hamstrings. Blood flowed off the ankle.

"Damn thing dinged me," she said. She rolled up the leg of the suit. A quarter-sized patch of skin had peeled off.

When the lesson ended, Henry asked, "Did you see me get up on the board?"

Everyone looked alike in the pictures, bright pink bodies in the murky water.

"Yes," she said. "Good job."

On the third day, she felt better, and they rented kayaks and a guide.

"You have a good stroke," Joshua, the guide, a young man just graduated from high school, told her.

They practiced in the bay.

"You're splashing me," Henry said from the back of the kayak.

They paddled by fish farms, rusting sheds floating on the water.

"Millions of fish get born there every day," Joshua said.

Their paddles got tangled in the sea cabbage, bulbous green orbs trailing ten-foot tendrils.

"You can eat them," Joshua said.

They paddled to an old-growth forest and tied up their kayaks to overhanging tree branches. They walked on cedar planks through the underbrush.

"This tree is nine hundred years old," Joshua said. He had shorn his hair, but his face was round and youthful, especially when he took off his sunglasses.

"Think about how much has happened since this tree was born."

The tree's top had withered but its lower trunk sprouted branches and leaves.

"It's worth a million dollars," he said. "That's why they wanted to cut it down, all of them."

"You can sure make a lot of cabinets out of that tree," Henry said.

On the water, Olivia tore a piece of the cabbage tendril and chewed it. Its dense flesh would not give between her teeth.

"It's salty," she said, and spat it out.

"Gross," Henry said.

Later at the pub, Henry ordered two Guinness and a bowl of mussels.

"Look." She showed Henry her palms, white and wrinkly, the blistered skin at the base of her fingers filling with puss.

"We'll toughen you up yet," he said.

Olivia sipped the beer.

"This tastes bitter," she said.

"You can live on Guinness and oranges. Everything you need," he said.

"I used to be a wrestler. In high school." She sipped again. "I went to school on scholarship."

The mussels arrived.

"Were you any good?"

"Provincial champion," she said. She dipped a corner of baguette into the sauce, tomato and basil and wine. She spooned out a mussel, split the shell, detached the meat, and dipped the shell into the broth.

"Mussels are the texture of organs," she said. "But they're popular."

"How would you know?"

Her throat felt fine.

"I've had tripe," she said.

A week before the wedding, Olivia gave him a personality test.

"It's Jungian in origin, and seventy questions. Just pick the answer you feel is right for you. There are no right or wrong answers." She had made poached eggs in diced tomatoes for breakfast. They pushed the plates to the side of the table.

"Are you routinized or spontaneous?"

"Is *routinized* even a word?"

"Do you have a routine?"

"Everyone does."

"Do you enjoy having a routine?"

"Put me down for spontaneous."

When they finished the test, he said, "I change my mind. Put me down for routinized."

He was an introverted, intuitive thinker, right on the cusp of perceiving and judging, a Rational.

"That's about right," he said.

"I'm an Idealist," she said, and he snorted.

"We're a good match," she said. "It would be better if one of us were extroverted."

Henry chewed the skin around his thumbnail. A crust of yolk had dried to his wrist.

"What is your greatest fear?" he asked.

He bit into the corner of his thumbnail.

"To run out."

"Of what?"

"I don't mean of something."

They left the car at the bar. Henry said he couldn't drive, and they were so close.

In their suite, Olivia changed in the bathroom, and Henry opened a bottle of wine. She had planned to wear the white lace slip on their wedding night. When she came out of the bathroom, Henry said, "You look like a bride," and he took her picture.

"Turn to the left," he said. "Lie down, look away from the camera, yes, like that."

They were hung over in the morning and walked to the car, drove to the marina to set off on a whale watching tour. She bought two cups of coffee that tasted like ash from the company office, and a couple of lemon Danishes.

"The dough is stale," Henry said on the boat. "But the lemon filling is good. Not too sweet."

Far away from the shore the boat stopped, and all the passengers, fifteen or so of them, filed onto the deck.

"There!" a woman said. She was middle-aged and wore an orange visor on top of her head. Everyone ran to her side of the boat.

"Is this safe?" Olivia asked. A scabby-backed whale punctured the surface of the water and disappeared.

"You can barely see it," Henry said, looking into the viewer.

A tail swooped up dripping black water that looked like diamonds. It smacked the surface and slipped back down.

"I got it!" Henry said, and whooped.

They waited on deck. Once, the woman in the visor called out she'd seen something, but it was a seagull on the water, scooping fish.

"The pamphlet said guaranteed sightings," a man said. He was with the woman wearing the visor.

The captain said they had to get going, they were on a schedule. Everyone went back inside, but Henry said he would ride on deck.

"Be careful," Olivia said.

She fell asleep with her neck bent to her shoulder. She dreamt about the whale, its back covered in black warts. She woke when her head smacked into the seat in front. The boat jerked and trembled, a child started to cry. She turned to Henry, but of course he wasn't there; he was on deck.

She bashed her knee getting out of her seat. The boat was rocking but the captain had killed the engine. She steadied herself hanging onto the seats, a passenger shouted, "Whoa!" and the child started to scream. She ducked her head to clear the top of the doorframe.

Later, she would take a leave from teaching. His body would wash ashore, and the activists would announce they hit a whale. She would meet his mother and learn he couldn't swim, and, with this woman, pour his ashes into the Pacific, his wish from childhood. She would pack up his house in Mayland Heights and sell off what she could. She would leave the city for a better job back east and meet her second husband and have children, two girls. Later, she would forget him for days, then weeks, then months at a time.

Bur first she walked to the back of the boat.

The still ocean belied the boat's turbulence, the horizon blurred with the sky, cloudless. The rush of wind was silence.

Familia

The invoices arrived on heavy stock paper, cream coloured and embossed with a stylized orchid, the wedding planner's logo.

"Aren't orchids for funerals?" Harris had asked Bibi when the first bill for centrepieces and stemware arrived that January.

"I don't know anything about this wedding." Bibi threw up her hands. She had been peeling a carrot, and a string of skin flew from the peeler and stuck to the stainless-steel fridge door. Harris smiled.

"You laugh, but that girl never listens to me. One of her colours is fuchsia." Bibi crunched the peeled carrot, chewed it with her mouth open.

The latest invoice, for linens, featured a

$2,500 line item listing silk dupioni table runners.

"This is getting out of hand," Harris said.

They sat on their deck, swatting insects.

"I've never seen such a bad summer for flies," Bibi said. She sipped white wine from a tumbler.

"What is duponi anyway?" Harris asked.

"Dupioni. It's Italian. There's one right there. Oh, you moved your arm."

"I can't very well swat at it with my teeth," Harris said.

He was drinking gin and soda with a lime. He squeezed the slice into his glass, sucked the juice from the rind, plopped the peel into the liquid.

"They can't live in that condo much longer," Bibi said.

"Let his father build him a house."

"Don't be cheap, Harris." Bibi went inside for more wine, and Harris swatted a mosquito. It escaped through the woven plastic, which was arranged to look like a fly.

"Get her on the phone," Bibi said, returning with a full glass and a can of repellent.

She started spraying, and Harris flattened a palm on his glass and shielded his eyes with his other. A mosquito buzzed by his ear, and even though Harris shook his head, it stung him on the lobe.

Bibi stopped spraying.

"Shit, he got me."

"You should have swatted him."

She picked up her phone, pressed a button, and held it to Harris.

They hadn't stained the patio yet that summer. The grey paint had chipped off underneath the table. Bibi had caught a sliver in her heel that June.

Marcella picked up on the last possible ring.

"Hello," she said. She sounded like she had gravel in her cheeks.

"What's the matter?" Harris asked.

Marcella started hiccupping, or she had been already before the phone rang.

She had always hiccupped after spankings. Harris had only delivered half a dozen in her childhood, each a trauma: she would fight back, punching and kicking and screaming. He spent half the punishment restraining the tiny flinging limbs. He gave the last one when she was six: Marcella had smashed the vase his parents gave them for a wedding present; a rose was cut into the frosted crystal. It stood alone on the coffee table in the living room, the room that was for decoration only. The vase was for show, too—no one had ever placed a flower inside it. He spanked her for that, and she choked on her sobs and saliva, and she couldn't gain breath, and he thought, I've killed her.

His mother had visited from Italy the next Christmas, and Marcella had told her to go back home and to shut up, and she stuck out her tongue, stained green and red from a candy cane, but still he wouldn't hit her.

"I'm calling off the wedding," Marcella said, and hiccupped.

"Don't be rash, Chelli," he said.

"He hasn't chosen his suit," Marcella said. The wedding was in three weeks.

"This excludes him from your love?" Harris asked.

He had spoiled her afterwards, half-heartedly taking away toys and then seeming blind when Snorf the elephant or Toto the giant mouse appeared in her bed the very same night.

He swallowed his drink, the gin diluted from the melting ice cubes.

"There's only one thing to do," she said.

He scratched at his fattening ear lobe.

"Wait, I'm on my way."

Their house looked towards the mountains, and every day as he drove to work at his accounting firm where he now managed people more than he manipulated figures, Harris thought of turning around and plucking a peak from the vista; they looked so small.

"Who will barbeque?" Bibi said.

"Let the meat marinate. Have a papaya."

He backed the Volvo out of the driveway and chewed a cherry-flavoured lozenge between his molars.

Between his house in the west suburbs of the city and the condo he had purchased for his daughter, Harris drove by two Babincourt Builders billboards. "Babincourt Builders: the best in building," they read. A bold block B shadowed the outline of a modern house, all impossible angles and thrusting slabs of concrete. Marcella had designed it and insisted they change the original tagline: "Babincourt Builders: the best in the west." Horatio, Frank's father, wanted to keep the word *best* somewhere in there, though.

Harris referred to Frank, her fiancé, as F squared when Marcella wasn't around. The family was Quebecois, the grandfather a bricklayer. Horatio came out west in the seventies, and now Babincourt Builders was a leading luxury home manufacturer in the city. Frank himself knew nothing about the trade; he and Marcella met in an MBA program.

"I'll give you a good deal," Horatio had said the first time the families got together. He had grinned, and two rows of wine-stained Chiclets appeared.

"We like our house just fine, thank you. Marcella was born here."

"Not on the dining room table I hope!" Horatio had slapped his chest and laughed.

"You know what I mean."

"I think he was just trying to make conversation," Bibi said later as they got ready for bed. She smoothed a glob of rose-scented cream across her cheeks and under her eyes.

"He's an asshole," Harris had said.

Traffic was light, most people were off in the mountains for the weekend, and Harris arrived in good time.

Marcella buzzed him up. Gimle, the miniature boxer, scratched at Harris's calves.

"Hey, down," she said. She held an unlit cigarette between her lips.

Gimle stopped scratching and started to lick. Angry hives goosebumped Harris's skin.

"We're on the balcony," she said. "Keep your

shoes on."

A coil of black feces rested on the otherwise white pee pad.

They sat on wooden fold-up chairs.

"Make sure you don't use that hibachi," Harris said. A gleaming silver orb with a handle on top like a bent antennae sat in the corner.

"It's a gift. One of Frank's idiot friends. Charcoal causes cancer anyway," she said.

She had picked up Gimle but passed him over to Harris when she lit the cigarette.

"Bleh, filter's wet."

The dog licked Harris's arm.

She had lobbied for pets all through childhood, but Harris's allergies were too terrible.

"He's hypoallergenic," she had said of Gimle, but Harris knew otherwise.

Now Harris scratched his arm.

"It's just the saliva," she said. Marcella's eyes were pink-rimmed, and her lips looked raw.

"Where is Frank?"

She tapped ash into a jar that once held marmalade. Three butts floated in black scummy water.

"We went to Montreal last weekend," she said. "For our stags."

"Together?"

"We travelled together," she said.

"No, I meant did you have your parties together."

She shook her head and dropped the cigarette into the jar, and it hissed and then sank.

Marcella had started smoking in university. She would quit and then start up for a week or two and then quit again, for years. When Harris had smoked, it was a good pack and a half a day.

"You want something to eat?"

"Are you eating?"

"I'll make a salad. Gimle, keep Grandpa company."

Harris pushed aside the dog's head every time it licked his arms. Finally he gave the dog his fingers to suck on.

When they bought the place, an empty lot sat south of the building. Now a red crane had been installed, and pylons placed around the lot.

When Marcella was eleven, the three of them went to visit family. By that time, his mother had died, so they went to visit Bibi's family near Rome. Bibi translated awkwardly—Harris had only a rudimentary knowledge, his father had been English—and they left the family to tour after two weeks.

Harris still carried the photograph of the

three of them in front of the Coliseum in his wallet.

"You know why the Coliseum is so dirty on this side?" he had asked Marcella after the middle-aged Texan took the shot.

"Because Mussolini built the road here, for war."

"He lacked foresight, not as smart as you." He had elbowed her, and she had laughed.

The day before, Bibi had offered her lap to Marcella on the crowded Spanish steps, and Marcella had said, "I would rather kill myself." Harris had arrived with melting pots of gelati, almond and pistachio flavoured, to a crying wife and aloof daughter.

Bibi had lost the fleshiness she had had in that photograph, and now she straightened her hair, which was still black but dyed.

Harris looked the most similar, just a little greyer, perhaps less slim. And Marcella was a woman now, taller and thinner. That summer, she had put on weight, a roll of flesh, which now seemed smaller than it had at the time, pressing up and over her jeans.

"She's eating too many sweets," Bibi had said, and Harris agreed. Aunts and cousins had piled cookies onto plates and placed them on doilied coffee tables. And, of course, there was the pasta and the gelato. The last week they bought watermelon slices instead and walked around and around the city.

"We've already seen the wedding cake building!" Marcella would lament.

"When's the next time you'll be in Rome?" Harris would ask.

That fall, she entered junior high and turned twelve. The gym teacher made them run laps around the school or, if it was raining, perform calisthenics, cross-training he called it, in the gym. She lost the weight by November.

"Thank god. It's too hard to be a fat kid," Harris had said one evening when Marcella was at a friend's.

"Especially for girls," Bibi agreed.

That May, the school called; a ninth-grader had found Marcella throwing up her lunch. A concerned friend came forward and told Mrs. Graham, the health teacher, that Marcella had been throwing up food since September.

Harris had held Marcella that night, and she seemed fine. Not sickly with rotting teeth or a burnt-out esophagus. She started seeing a therapist, Joanne, and the vomiting, everyone agreed, stopped.

One night Marcella yelled, "I'm moving out when I'm eighteen! Joanne said those are my rights," and Bibi had said, "That childless hippie knows nothing about love."

Harris had told Bibi not to hover around Marcella's bathroom door after every meal. But the therapy continued until the end of grade nine, and all seemed fine.

"You want a glass of red?" Marcella came to the balcony with the wine already poured.

"It won't kill me." He took the glass from her and shifted Gimle, who was dozing, away from the table.

In grade ten, she bussed across the city to attend a bilingual program and lost all her friends. At Christmas that year, she sat cross-legged, shaking presents. She wore red flannel pyjamas with white candy canes dancing across them. She unwrapped, carefully, a box that Harris knew contained a cashmere sweater, her first, from Santa.

Underneath the pyjamas she wore a pair of long johns. The layers folded sharply over her knees.

"Ohmygod, ohmygod, I love it!" She lifted

the sweater above her head. The soft brown would offset her eyes. Harris had chosen it at Holt's, and when he brought it home, Bibi had said, "You spoil that girl."

"Are you cold?" he asked Marcella then.

She flushed to match the pants and set her lips in a straight line, cheeks hollowing as she did so. She took breakfast in her room, saying she felt dizzy. "Nauseous," she'd said. Harris flinched when Bibi said, "You mean nauseated."

She hung around the kitchen all afternoon as her mother and aunts cooked the turkey. "I'll do the gravy," she said. They all praised her gravy and the potatoes she whipped. She took a slice of turkey breast, a spoonful of potatoes, stuffing, and half a dozen Brussels sprouts. She spent dinner in and out of the kitchen, delivering serving spoons and carving knives, sopping up her little cousins' spills, and her plate disappeared before Harris could confirm she had eaten anything at all.

After Christmas, she stopped eating red meat, then white. Fish was next, then eggs, dairy. She ran each morning, waking well before dawn. If Harris left for work early enough, he sometimes saw her, limbs like naked branches weighed down by fleece.

Next, rice, pasta, and bread. She ate broth, vegetable soup, grapefruits, but only alone. She had volleyball practice, or track, or she was studying, or she had eaten a huge dinner, always a huge dinner, with teammates.

In the spring, the bones in her face began to protrude: the bridge of her nose, eye sockets, the sheath of her forehead.

By July, a fine fur had started to grow on her cheeks. She wore turtle necks, layered one on another, and sweatpants over sweatpants.

One afternoon in August, Harris brought her a piece of toast. It was dry; he knew better than to spread the thinnest layer of butter.

"Please eat this," he said. She lay on her side in a nest on her bed, duvet arranged around her fragile frame, her shrinking head and child hands poking out of the sports clothes she was now too weak to run in. She looked like a newly born bird.

"I can't."

"You mean you won't."

That night, she fainted in the bathroom, hit her head on the sink. The gash bled over Bibi in the back seat, who kept saying, "Wake up, Chelli, wake up."

Harris ran three red lights on the way to the hospital.

She would stay in the psych ward, and the whole family would participate in therapy.

"She weighs sixty-seven pounds," Dr. Freeman said. "Don't tell her that," and then, "But I've seen worse."

"Do you like quinoa?" Marcella set two plates on the table, forks stuck into the green, red, and yellow salads.

"The little brown things that look like insect pods?"

"Ha ha. Gimle, down."

Harris placed Gimle on the floor, and the dog settled at his feet.

They crunched through the red peppers and cucumbers. Poppy seeds from the dressing stuck in his teeth.

"Everything's from the farmer's market."

"I feel healthier already," Harris said.

She was still wearing her engagement ring, a blinding solitaire Frank had bought in New York.

She sighed and sipped wine.

"Okay, Chelli, I got a bill for some duponi. That's why I called."

She chewed on her lip and then said: "We

went to the strippers. I went to the male strippers, he went to the female strippers." She pulled a cigarette from the pack on the table and reached for the little jar she had set on the balcony floor.

"And you're upset that he went to the strippers?"

"The strippers were really lame. They danced in angel outfits and firefighter hats, but they didn't take their clothes off. It was pointless. All the men there were, I bet you anything, gay, and all these women were just ready to rape them. Men dressed as angels, men in firemen's hats. What's wrong with people?

"Anyway, my friends got me drunk, his friends got him drunk, it was all very egalitarian, you know?"

Gimle had fallen asleep and was leaning against Harris's foot. The dog breathed rhythmically.

"I threw up on the sidewalk, he got a lap dance. He told me the next morning that he got a lap dance. His buddies bought it for him. He said that the girl looked okay from far away but that up close her eyes were wrinkled, and she smelled like smoke."

She took a drag and shrugged.

"I mean, who cares, you know? This is what

people do."

When the construction to the south of the building finished, Marcella's view of downtown would be partially blocked.

"The next day we went downtown. We were so hung over, we wanted pho, but you can't find pho in that city except for in this one restaurant in Chinatown."

"Pho?"

"Vietnamese soup. Really, Dad? Anyway, we have to take the metro because we're too sick to walk, and while we're waiting on the platform, this guy who looks kind of fucked-up staggers a bit and then pulls out his, you know, and starts peeing, but he starts to pee on a man sitting on the benches."

"On purpose?"

"Not on purpose; the guy was probably on drugs. He was messed up. So the man sitting on the benches yells and pushes him away, and the man falls but keeps peeing, on himself, and then the man who was sitting starts to kick him. Really kick him. In the stomach, the face, the back, and the peeing man starts to wake up a bit and yell, but the kicking doesn't stop. The guy can't move, there's blood everywhere, I'm screaming, and then the kicker pees on the man he just beat up."

Ash from her cigarette fell to her lap.

"It sounded like a ball hitting a bat, but it was his nose and then his jaw, his ribs, his legs."

Marcella's voice was steady, practiced. She balanced on the back of her chair with her feet resting on the railing and brushed the ash from her jeans.

"Frank didn't do anything. I said help him, but he didn't do anything. It happened fast. Security came, and then our metro came, and we got on and that was it.

"But at the restaurant, after we ordered our soup, he started laughing. He said that guy didn't see it coming, what an asshole, and he laughed and laughed.

"I said what do you mean, and he said the guy got what he deserved. Our soup came, we ate it, and later that day we met our friends, and he told the story to them, and he said again that the guy deserved it."

"And that's it?"

"That's everything. What more could there be?"

In therapy, Dr. Freeman told Bibi and Harris that Marcella's disease was a symptom of the family. A woven tapestry hung above the doctor's desk, a rural scene depicting the collection of rice, small black-haired people stooping in a green field. It looked Peruvian to Harris, although he'd never been.

"Are you saying that we don't love her enough, that we made her do this?" Bibi asked.

"It's a form of suicide, and a call for help," Dr. Freeman said. "The biggest problem is that she doesn't believe herself lovable."

"It seems the biggest problem is she weighs less than an eight-year-old," Bibi said. She started to cry, grabbed for a tissue off the coffee table and upset a red clay pot. It rolled from side to side on the table, like a bug that couldn't right itself, until the doctor picked it up and placed it on his desk.

"What do we do?" Harris asked.

"We feed her and convince her that she's wrong," Dr. Freeman said.

But Marcella wouldn't cooperate. The nurses reported that she spat juice back into the glass and exercised at night; they'd caught her doing sit-ups in her hospital bed, tricep lunges on the visitor's chair.

Harris bought flowers every day, first from the gift store on the main level by the emergency ward and then from the Safeway adjacent to the hospital. Arrangements of gerbers, carnations, lilies, summer mixes with berries proliferated and filled Marcella's corner, her roommate's bedside table, the nurses' reception desk, the TV room.

"You're cheering the place up," a nurse named Prea told him. He did not foster the flowers after drop off, but they were well cared for: no festering water or wilting petals.

"We love you, Marcella," he would say when he arrived. She would sit and stare out the window or at her hands. An IV was sunk into her right forearm, and sometimes she scratched at it without purpose. He brought a book to read, or the paper, and stayed until the PA said visiting time was over.

One day, Harris brought a crib board and cards, an autumn harvest bouquet of sunflowers; it was already fall.

He'd had the set for decades.

"You want to get to fifteen," he said.

"Coleen tried to kill herself today," Marcella said. The skin around her lips was red. Her hair, which had curled tightly in spirals before, had thinned and straightened itself; it hung limp and unwashed around her face.

"She sliced her wrists with metal from the bed. I heard the nurses talking."

Coleen was a depressive and slept behind the drawn curtain most of the time. She accepted hand-me-down bouquets, but she had never spoken when Harris was around.

"They took her to emerg," she said. "I hope she's okay."

"I'm sure she's fine. Maybe it was for attention."

Harris shuffled the deck and it made a slurping sound.

Marcella licked her lips.

"It's not for attention," she said.

He'd lost the blue pegs decades earlier and replaced them with twigs of spaghetti. Marcella snapped hers, breaking it between thumb and forefinger.

"Do you think she'll die?"

"Marcella, please."

"Do you think I will?" She licked her lips again. She'd been a nail biter before, ripping off the white tips, chewing the skin raw to bleeding around the nail beds. He kissed her on the forehead and left.

"Have you told Frank?"

"He's buying suits."

"But you haven't told him."

"He thinks it's because he hasn't bought the suits. What's wrong with your ear?"

Harris rubbed the lobe; it began to itch and burn again.

"What should I do about the tablecloths?" Harris asked.

The dog napped on her lap, their wine glasses stood empty.

"Nothing," Marcella said. "I'll call and cancel. I'll pay back the deposits."

She placed the dog on the floor and went inside and brought out the bottle of wine.

"It's not about the money," he said. He waved away the bottle, but she splashed a sip into his glass. "Love is never certain, Chelli."

Harris lifted the dog into his lap.

"My view will be blocked when they finish building that," she said.

The dog started to growl.

"Gimle does this every night at this time, don't you, killer?"

Harris stayed away a full week. He had told Bibi he was spending long hours at work, and when he returned to the hospital, he brought two dozen pink roses. A glass of white daisies in soupy water still languished on the nurses' desk.

Coleen lay napping, her wrists wrapped in bleached gauze. On the other side of the curtain, Marcella sat up in bed, reading a second-hand paperback.

She looked up and said, "I want to go back to school." A squeezed juice box, grape flavoured, rested on her tray. "I want to get out of here."

He was so pleased to hear it, he said, and they loved her. He said he'd been busy with work. She dropped her head into the book, a strand of loose hair falling into her line of vision. She brushed it away and moved her lips as she read.

Dr. Freeman confirmed she'd started eating: a handful of grapes, a cup of applesauce, a spoonful of rice pudding. Not much, but not nothing, he said—a start. They could take out the IV soon.

"Don't mention the food," he said. "Sometimes it sticks, sometimes it doesn't."

Gimle jumped out of Harris's lap and ran to the front door, barking. It clicked open and closed, and Frank padded towards them, the dog jumping up on his hind legs, skipping around his master.

"The other suits are on order." Frank stood in the doorway to the balcony. "They arrive on Thursday." He held a garment bag in one hand and a shoebox in the other.

"Sir." Frank nodded to Harris, and Harris stood and nodded back.

"I'll pay for the tablecloths," he said. "You two sort this out."

Frank's face had softened, like melting Jell-O. Marcella was looking in the direction of the crane, squeezing her lips together. Harris let himself out.

Harris called Bibi in the car; she had already grilled the meat and drunk the wine.

"I'll stop at the office, get some of the paperwork together," he said.

"I'm in a coma," she said.

In the days before the internet, Harris had always just called the agency; he'd ask for a blonde, or a brunette, or he'd ask by name if he found a favourite.

They still used a suite downtown, its kitchen pristine, the sheets crisp and of a high thread count. Blue swirls patterned the duvet.

He parked the car easily. Everyone had abandoned the city for the mountains.

He'd met with Michelle once or twice before. She'd chosen her name well: her face was shaped like a heart and she dyed her hair a realistic auburn. Her eyes looked unnaturally green.

He asked for a massage, and she rubbed him inexpertly, pulling the skin of his shoulders, but he refused the offer of lotion even though it was scent-free. She started to massage his thighs, and he stopped her; she was pulling on the hairs.

"Who cleans this place?" he asked, removing his watch.

"I don't know." She took off her bra. Her nipples pointed to the sides, her breasts small handfuls but real.

"Wait," he said. "Close the drapes."

They were twenty stories up and downtown was lit. The mountains, just in front of them, were invisible.

"Okay," he said, and she walked to him.

He had called Dr. Freeman after Marcella returned home with an official weight of 105. She spent evenings in her room, studying and whispering into the phone. She would earn a scholarship, leave home at eighteen, regrow her hair, become lean and strong.

"We did this to her," he said.

"No," the doctor said. "It's a mystery."

Already they were satellites.

The Jesus Year

Three weeks before Erica's Jesus year, Barry said they weren't throwing a party.

"No one has parties for their thirty-third birthday." He brushed a curl of dog hair from his shoulder.

"Some people do. Some people have a party every year."

They had not thrown a party for Erica's thirty-second birthday, either. Liam, her brother, had taken a fall. There were no parties that year.

Erica started going to the gym two weeks into her thirty-second year, shortly after her mother sent her an email whose subject line read: "Why keep aspirin by your bedside: About Heart Attacks." The email said:

Why keep aspirin by your bedside?
About Heart Attacks

There are other symptoms of an heart attack besides *the pain on the left arm*.
One must also be aware of *an <u>intense pain on the chin</u>*, as well as <u>*nausea* and lots of *sweating*</u>.

The majority of people (about 60%) who had a heart attack during their sleep, did not wake up.
However, if it occurs, the chest pain may wake you up from your deep sleep.
If that happens, *immediately dissolve two aspirins in your mouth* and swallow them with a bit of water.
Afterwards: CALL 911
- *say "heart attack!"*
- *say that you have taken 2 aspirins..*
- DO NOT lie down

Erica didn't bother with the aspirin. She stripped bare and saw a prehistoric fertility goddess statue, the kind found in caves: oblong breasts, bloated tummy, distended pubis. Erica read health articles; she knew about toxic gut fat and the insidious nature of type 2 diabetes. She grasped her belly for the sprouting of tumours. She joined the gym the next day.

A taxi driver, the one witness, saw Liam punch a man outside Diego's Saloon and start a run. The taxi driver said he never saw a man move so fast.

Liam ran so fast he did not notice the caution tape or the pylons. He ran so fast he ran into a four-storey deep construction pit that would become the city's tallest building. They had poured concrete that morning.

They found her brother Monday, cast in the concrete, and they had to break it up and pry his body from what would become the parkade, and this made the cover of the local newspaper. In mourning, Erica had to listen to inane disc jockeys joke about swan dives and concrete shoes, except they weren't shoes, it was a concrete coffin, ha ha, ha ha.

His actual casket was closed, but someone had to confirm it was Liam that was dead, and the task fell to Barry. He muttered in his sleep for weeks after, ripping the sheets off her body and burying his sleeping face in them.

Erica started with five-pound dumbbells and bicep curls. She speed-walked on the treadmill. After six visits, she employed Mikey, the resident trainer.

"That a girl—do it! Yeah! Two more reps—yeah! One more—yeah!"

Erica focused on Mikey's Adam's apple, a sharp bump bobbing in the striations of his neck. She doubled the weight, tripled the number of reps. Fibres ripped and knit together, scarred. At night, Erica's blood pulsed.

Barry explained they would *celebrate* her birthday. He called Marcutio's. In the fruit bowl on the counter, a mango had split along its side and browned juice glued the skin to the pastel ceramic. Marcutio's used to be Erica's favourite restaurant. Now she would prefer the vegetarian bistro on 1st that served the spicy green coconut hot pot, but she is the only one who would enjoy it.

"Saturday, eight o'clock, for five."

Erica started to say six, and stopped.

After the funeral, Barry squeezed Erica's waist in the kitchen. Her pants were wool but lined—they were the only pants she could wear; they were black. The waistband was not lined, and her stomach itched where he squeezed her.

"Fucking Darwin awards," Barry said.

Erica would agree that Liam ate glass shards when he was five; that he set the living room curtains on fire when she turned twelve, on purpose, with a lighter; that he smashed his head into the bathroom mirror the day before his Math 30 exam, three times, she could hear them, before he passed out; that he drove an uninsured Mazda off Crowchild Trail and landed tires down on Memorial Drive and tried to keep driving except that the engine block was cracked.

"We need to brush the dog," she said.

Erica bought a new pair of running shoes; the old pair wore out. She rounded the gym twice every visit, lunging with a twenty-five-pound weight in each hand. Mikey cheered her on, high-fived at her weigh-ins. When she worked out alone, she swore herself into action: Fuck yeah. Goddamn, awesome. Shit hell, and the like.

At the restaurant, the hostess seated them at a round table so that everyone had to look at each other. When Erica's plate of grilled Pacific salmon on wilted spinach arrived, she poured salt over half of it.

"You look sharp," Simone said. As Erica's oldest friend, she remembered that Marcutio's was Erica's favourite restaurant.

"Erica has always been tenacious." Her mother stirred her ice water with the butter knife.

"Erica was planning on going to law school." Her father sliced his steak with the fork in his right hand.

"Erica is never at home; she's with her trainer at that gym all the time." Barry started choking on his mouthful of Parmesan chicken.

"I wanted a party," Erica said, and Barry

wrapped his hands around his throat, and they listened to the choking sounds.

A Raising

Viv drives the thirty kilometres from the deep southwest every Sunday to brunch with her daughter. The time they tried the Humpty's in Viv's neighbourhood, Tabitha ordered brown toast and sent it back when it came buttered.

Tabitha runs, every morning, even Sundays. Even if she didn't, she could never be plump; her body is not built that way.

Viv adds her name to the wait list and sits on a concrete planter outside the adjacent cardiology clinic. Petunias wilt in the heat, their home of soil is grey and cracked. The diner, a place called Locale, serves small portions of locally sourced produce, meat, and eggs. When Viv lights the cigarette, a dozen waiting patrons disperse, leaving behind a boozy cloud and the scent of unwashed skin.

Tabitha is training for a marathon, her twelfth. This one she had to qualify for. She'll have to go down to the States to run it. Every time she talks about the running, Viv says, "Who's chasing you?"

Tabitha could have modelled. Not high fashion, but at least catalogues. Viv never mentioned it, and Tabitha never asked; perhaps it hadn't occurred to her.

When Tabitha was fourteen, she showed her mother a picture of Kate Moss in an old issue of Vogue her friend had passed on to her. The model was half nude, not just her body, her face naked and blazing.

"Everyone's beautiful when they're young," Viv had said. "I was beautiful."

It wasn't true. Viv's eyes are hooded and have always been. Her mouth turns down at the sides, and spit collects in the corners; they are always moist, as though she has been or will be sick. She tans her skin from a pale ash to cheerful orange three days a week. She bought a bed after catching a fungal infection off an improperly sanitized surface at the salon.

It is July and already hot at ten. Viv chain-smokes. The skin around her lips has creased like antique paper or crumpled silk. The sun pierces through her thinning auburn curls, cut tight to her head, right to her scalp. If only she looked good in hats.

She has painted her toenails a brown-hued taupe. They are skinny, like claws on the paw of a dog. Viv has to trim back the tough skin, like hide, that grows on the nail bed and over the edge of her toes. The skin never bleeds.

When Tabitha was a teenager, they would go to the mall and eat at the food court, and Viv would ask, "What about that one?" and point to a woman, and Tabitha would say, always, "She's pretty."

"That one?" Viv would say of a teenaged girl with a pixie cut. "She'll have jowls like a turkey in ten years." Or, "Her?" and she would point to a twenty-five-year-old wearing a deep V-neck showing off buoyant cleavage and say, "Her tits will hang to her toes by thirty."

When Tabitha was fifteen, Viv booked a vacation in Mexico for Christmas. Doris at the office was always bringing back miniature sombreros and little bottles of tequila.

They stayed for cheap at an all-inclusive and

were given blue plastic bracelets like hospital tags that had to be worn 24/7 and could only be removed with scissors. At the buffet, where they ate every meal, Viv would say, "Load up," but Tabitha took half spoonfuls of bean salad and rice. Everything tasted salty and of fish, even, it seemed, the breakfast cereal.

The resort had a thin strip of beach, but Viv didn't trust the water. They sat by the pool and Viv took the ten a.m. swimmercize class taught by Etan, the resort's chestnut-skinned fitness instructor. Tabitha hid under an umbrella, she burned easily, and Viv drank gin and tonics out of plastic glasses throughout the afternoons. She tipped the server, Rocco, and told him to take care of her. He brought her fresh drinks and took away the glasses she stacked underneath the plastic reclining bed.

Before lunch buffet was served, the staff gathered in front of the pool to lip-sync a song in English and perform a choreographed dance.

"Sunrise Bay, we're here for you, Sunrise Bay, we love what we do," they would mouth.

Etan joined in at the front. He did not sing but led the dance, the hand twirls and grapevines. His nipples, two pink push-pins, bounced neatly on his chest.

"That is a fine specimen," Viv would say each day.

On the seventh and final night, Tabitha went missing. Viv alerted management, who organized a search party. Their flashlights found Etan and Tabitha kissing on the beach. They would discover back home that the sand had stained Tabitha's white skirt all along the back.

Tabitha walks to the diner each week, she lives so close. She can walk everywhere, to work downtown, to the organic Italian grocer, to the pathway system on which she runs. She and her husband, Hume, have done this on purpose and talk about it every Christmas in Viv's townhouse. When Viv bought the place, dark cedar was in fashion.

Today Tabitha walks straight-backed, head bobbing from three blocks away. Her long blonde hair is wet. It will dry smooth and straight without fly-aways.

"You're late," Viv says when Tabitha reaches her. Tabitha kisses her on the cheek, a dry peck, stands back and wrinkles her nose.

"I told you, it was a long run today."

The hostess, a thin young woman with black hair spun into a bun on the top of her head, calls Viv's name, and they follow her inside.

Tabitha says, "Perfect timing." When they sit, lucky to get the table by the open window, she says, "Oh, Mom, your feet."

It was Viv's brother who wrecked them. She was seven, and Richard took a brick from a pile in the backyard. The bugs they loved so much had left squiggly marks on its underside. As he turned the brick over, it slipped from his fingers, landed squarely on her toes, which broke, along with a metatarsal in her left foot. The nails fell out, and Richard got a beating. He wheeled her around the backyard in an office chair for the rest of the summer. Where else did they have to go?

The nails grew back funny but strong and thick.

Viv orders coffee with cream and the farmer's breakfast: three eggs sunny side up, old-fashioned sausage, potatoes, and sauerkraut. Tabitha has the vegan special: roasted tofu and curried vegetables, green tea included.

"We're thinking of going somewhere hot this winter," Tabitha says when the drinks come. She stirs her tea without clanging the sides of the glass, even though she has put nothing in it.

"Hume says Jamaica, I say Aruba," Tabitha laughs.

The diner serves pressed coffee, a strong,

thick brew. Viv adds two packs of sugar and the entire mini carafe of cream. She will ask for more when the waitress returns.

"I was thinking of taking a trip myself," Viv says. She folds the empty sugar packets into tiny squares. "That place we went to in Mexico that one time was nice."

"Didn't they make the staff sing some stupid song?"

"You liked the fitness leader well enough."

The food arrives. A translucent skin rests atop Viv's eggs. She does not like them overcooked.

"Who?" Tabitha pushes the cubes of tofu and sliced pepper spears around her plate, lifting them and looking underneath.

"You know who," Viv says, gives a short laugh.

"Oh, Mom, I was a kid," she says. "I need hot sauce, but not that Tabasco stuff. Can you get the waitress when she comes?"

Viv salts and peppers her eggs, pulls apart her toast, and bursts a yolk with a piece of crust.

"This might be our last chance to have some time to ourselves," Tabitha says, nibbling on a wedge of speared tofu and smiling.

When Tabitha was an infant, barely walking, Doug, Tabitha's father, locked Viv out in the snow. She was brining the turkey for Christmas, and Doug was drinking three-quarter-rum eggnogs. He came around for a sloppy kiss as she was manoeuvring the carcass in its pot, and she splashed his drink with the salted turkey water. He pushed her out the door, locked it, and disappeared, down into the basement. Viv went around the house, rattling glass and kicking at the doors. Little Tabitha followed from door to window to door, smacking her doughy palms against all the surfaces, a one-sided game of patty cake. When night descended, Viv got hold of her mind and went to the neighbours, called the police, and, after a little while, divorced Doug, found a job, filed for custody, and so on.

Christmas day, her big toenails began to throb and burn. On New Year's, a night spent with popcorn, vodka sodas, and cough syrup for the child, they popped off for the second time.

"You said you wanted chilli sauce?" Viv says. The waitress stands at the table to ask about the first few bites.

"Do you have yellow habanero sauce?" Tabitha asks the waitress. To Viv she says, "I'm thinking we'll both take leave, me first, Hume second."

Viv had given Tabitha her last name, Lamar,

a name she had invented, and then when Tabitha married Hume, she took Jeffers. If Doug had had his way, Tabitha would be a Tamara, Tamara Jeffers, a woman Viv has never met, thirty, married, pregnant, not a wrinkle on her face.

"What do you think of this one?" Viv says to the waitress, who has arrived with the sauce. "What do you think?"

Hasard

"An IT professional," Julie answered for George. He claimed two glasses of red from a passing waiter's tray.

"Continual Service Improvement, actually," George said. They were talking to a poet, Pierre, who was tapping a cigarette, filter down, into his palm.

"And I'm a Crown prosecutor, tax fraud," Julie said.

She sipped the wine, a Bordeaux, and sucked in her cheeks.

Pierre lifted his cigarette into the air and walked to the terrace.

"Little prick," she said. "How do Angela and

Derek know such a person?"

"Just give me a moment," George said, and left her standing alone.

Angela threw a Christmas party every year, and Julie always came. A decade earlier, Angela had served vegan chili out of mismatched mugs, and everyone had sat on the floor, passing joints and drinking cans of Pabst Blue Ribbon.

"Chère Julie." Angela appeared behind Julie and pressed a cool palm against Julie's neck. Her angora sweater stuck to the sweat between her shoulder blades.

"What a beautiful party," Julie said. White candles, a foot around and four feet high, blazed around the perimeter of the giant living room. Red lamps tippled light up the walls.

"Aren't you worried something will catch on fire?"

"Have a canapé." Angela pinched a cracker with rolled smoked salmon stuffed with capers and cream cheese from another roving tray. She tilted her head, and her face fell into light. A pouch of bruised skin swelled out from the brow bone and drifted to the cheek.

"Jesus, Ange," Julie said.

"It was stupid. I slipped down the stairs." She patted her knee. "Everything's swollen. I can't even do Pilates."

"You could have cancelled."

"And disappoint everyone?" Angela's mouth was already stained purple. "Where is gorgeous George?" she asked.

"Oh for god's sake, he still has asthma, doesn't he remember?"

George was outside on the terrace, smoking a cigarette with the poet.

"I'm surprised he isn't wearing a beret," Julie said. A skewered shrimp passed by.

"He's a cousin."

"Yours?" Julie had known Angela's family for fourteen years, since university.

"From Virginia," she said.

"Where is Derek?" A crash and a tinkling of glass came from the kitchen.

"Maryanne's here; keep her company," Angela said, and followed the noise.

Pierre did write poetry, prose poems collated into what he called chapbooks. He had given Angela one, typed on recipe cards and held together with splintered chopsticks and green twist ties, delivered it to her office a week after she assessed him.

He'd never started the therapy, though, and only wanted to visit her.

When she and Derek bought the place, a three level hugging the mountain, they gutted the kitchen. The original oven had been too small to hold a roasting pan. They'd ripped out drywall to expose the century-old brick and demolished a pantry. Still, it felt snug, so they hung pots and pans from the ceiling above the island to save space. Now the pots lay in a pile on top of the bananas in the fruit bowl shaped like a hollowed apple, a gift from Angela's mother-in-law. It had cracked in two.

"So sorry, Madam," Sève the caterer said. "It just fell."

The rack had been screwed into a wooden beam.

"It's not your fault," Angela said. "Can you start serving the asparagus quiche?"

"Right away, Madam."

Angela poured a glass of Valpolicella, her own bottle. Derek would only drink French wine from Bordeaux. He stored his bottles in the special room behind his den. If Angela felt like wine, she took a trip to the SAQ.

"Here, Madam." Sève presented her with a two-bite quiche on a gold-rimmed white plate.

She shook her head. They'd done a tasting the week before. A female server picked up a tray, and Angela drank half the glass before setting it down again.

When Pierre had brought the chapbook, almost a year ago now, she'd told him she couldn't accept gifts from students.

"It's not a gift," he said. "You said in our session my creative focus is key."

"It was an assessment, not a session," she said. "I am not your therapist."

She was a psychologist, but after her promotion, she handled intake, organized the other therapists, managed their breakdowns.

"Then we can be friends," he said.

The next week, he appeared again at her door. She booked the hour in her calendar, marked it private.

"I wanted to be a poet," he said. "But I'm a coward."

"You're writing now, though."

"I have a plan. Degree, job. The writing is second. I am too scared."

He grew a proper beard and looked older than twenty-four. His hair greyed over his ears.

"I wanted to be an actress," she said. "But I was terrible. And then I became this." She gestured to her office. "And then I wanted to be a mother."

"You are a mother."

"Teya's everything," she said.

Before the party, she scoffed three extra-strength gel caplets to numb her face, and the wine, its warmth trickling into the bottom of her belly, started doing its job.

She drained the rest of the glass.

"You smell like an ashtray," Julie said.

"It's a party," George said.

"Quiche?" Another tray appeared.

"No. Well, wait." Julie placed the quiche in her palm. When she bit into it, the crust crumbled in her mouth. It tasted of butter and rosemary.

"That Pierre guy *is* a poet," George said. "He's got a book coming out."

"I'm sure it will be wildly popular."

"And why is pursuing a passion such a bad thing?"

"Oh, shit." Julie took another bite of the pastry, and half of it fell to the floor.

Maryanne approached, her belly the size of a barrel, bulging out of her navy peacoat.

"I'm a whale," she said. Julie kissed her on both cheeks. Maryanne's skin smelled citrusy; under the floral alcohol of hairspray, her hair was unwashed.

"When's the big day?"

"Tuesday, which is the thirteenth, so I'm hoping to either squeeze it out on the Monday or hold on. Freddy is on parental duty tonight."

All three of them had thrown out their birth control at the same time. Angela's daughter, Teya, was five now. It had taken Maryanne three years to conceive. This second one, though, surprised them.

"I will never tell it that. What if it thought we only wanted Taylor?" At the time, she was four months pregnant. She had grasped the hard bowl of her belly.

"How am I this big, when the little shit is the size of a bean?"

One of the tri-wicked candle flames reached a foot in the air. Smoke poured up from the blue tip.

"Have many citizens defrauded the government of its due recently?"

"I spent all week in court. This family from Mumbai brought over $50,000 of undeclared jewellery. The four-year-old boy was wearing three necklaces."

"Ballsy. Is that cheese?"

Julie picked a wedge of soft cheese on a cracker.

"I am so jealous, you are drinking wine. I would kill for a fucking margarita and a piece of brie."

Julie had forgotten about her glass.

"Have a sip," she said.

Maryanne lifted her eyebrows.

"Just kidding."

Maryanne had been Angela's friend from high school. It had been Angela's idea to try together.

"It's now or never," she had said, although they all thought they had a lot of time. They got together at Angela and Derek's and drank three bottles of wine, took pictures of each other dancing and making duck faces for the camera.

"I think I got knocked up that night," Angela had said.

"I need to put my coat somewhere," Maryanne said.

"I have to find the lady's room," Julie said.

"I wonder if it's in the same place," Maryanne said. "They're always changing something around here."

Angela had told Pierre not to come to the party. He had wanted to get together on the weekend. He would be away over Christmas, and he wouldn't let her be until she told him why exactly she was busy.

He was one of the first guests to arrive. She had left him alone to chain-smoke on the terrace.

Now she poured herself another glass of wine and a pint of water. She chugged the water and her belly ached from the volume; she was slight.

He had first been to the house that summer.

She had called him the day before their informal appointment to cancel. Everyone in the office was away, and it was hot.

"Let's meet for a coffee," he had said.

She brought a work notebook to the meeting. They sat inside in spite of the heat, sipping iced lattes, which she paid for.

"Everyone loves summer so much, it oppresses me," he said, and slurped up the last of the coffee. "I think about school all summer long, about the anxiety I will feel in September, which makes me anxious."

"Mindfulness," Angela said. "It's a practice where you concentrate on the moment, where you focus on the present, the now."

"I feel that way with you," he said.

He raked his fingers through his hair, which was limp and greasy in the humidity.

They walked afterwards; she was steering, it was her neighbourhood.

This is reckless, she thought. They ended up at her door. She said, "Oh, this is where I live," like it was a surprise.

"I'm thirsty."

"Come on then."

She gave him a tour and they reached the loft, which was hers.

"I would create a studio here!"

She wondered, haven't I? The space was utilitarian: a desk and chair, a shelf of books she had installed herself. A potted plant and a picture of Teya, newborn and wrinkled, on the desk. A sheepskin on the floor, on which she meditated.

"Here I would put an easel," Pierre said, framing a space in the corner with his fingers. "And here, bookshelves. So much space," he said. He walked to the window and leaned against the ledge.

Underneath his T-shirt, his torso narrowed in a slim V. The muscles in his shoulders flexed and released as he rocked against the ledge.

"Come away," she said.

His beard prickled her cheeks when they kissed. She couldn't remember having slept with a twenty-four-year-old. Derek had been older, twenty-eight, when they met.

When they finished, Pierre asked, "Can I stay?"

They lay their heads on the sheepskin.

Derek was away at a conference, and Teya was at her grandmother's. She would return from the country talking only of horses.

"For a little while," Angela said.

Julie had sent a bouquet the afternoon of the party. Years before, when Angela and Derek had their first catered soirée, Julie hadn't known, and she and George brought a bottle of wine.

Derek had sold a tech start-up, acquired another one, and so on and so on.

"Will you stop working?" she'd asked Angela after the first sell.

Teya was just one and in daycare.

"And lose my mind?" They had laughed and clinked espressos.

At that party, nobody served their wine. Julie snuck into the kitchen late, and the bottle was still wrapped in a red Christmas bow, looking ridiculous next to the uniform bottles of vintage Bordeaux, little orange seals marking their pedigree.

Angela, or perhaps the housekeeper, had put the bouquet in the bathroom. Green berries punctuated the white roses.

Julie's nose shone; she took out a powder compact from her party handbag, a rectangle of snakeskin that she tucked under her armpit.

The day before, she'd eaten lunch at the Italian deli in the basement of the government building.

She'd ordered a salad; she was watching her weight, but it was a Caprese. She ate the bocconcini first.

The anti-diet book she was reading said to "treasure pleasure." Define your pleasure and indulge, in small quantities, and not every day. More than that, find pleasure in quality. Eschew sugar-laden milk chocolate, margarine, fried chicken, processed meat.

The salad had marinated in a goopy balsamic reduction, and the cheese had turned brown. She sliced the balls in three with the edge of her fork.

A mother and toddler claimed the seat next to her.

"Amelia, stop fussing," the mother said.

Julie speared chickpeas and plopped them in

her mouth.

The toddler, dressed in a magenta snowsuit, the hood pulled up around her face, breathed around a pacifier. She hit the table with her fists.

"Amelia, I'm warning you."

The woman had removed her hat and scarf and unzipped her puffy white bomber, brown around the cuffs.

The toddler spat out her pacifier onto the table, and the woman wiped it against her pants, plopped it into her own mouth and back into the child's.

Julie stabbed her plate; she'd finished the salad unaware. The book said to concentrate on every bite and every swallow.

And yet this mother, reading the English weekly and ignoring her daughter, was rail thin, a cinched belt pleating corduroy at her waist.

The toddler started to scream around the soother, spat it out again, her cheeks purple and hot-looking. The mother slapped the girl's hand.

"She's hot, just take off the suit," Julie said.

"Who asked you?"

"Any idiot can see that she's suffocating."

The child stopped screaming, her mouth an O of shock.

"Who the fuck do you think you are?"

Julie gathered her bag and jogged to the security kiosk by the entrance to the law library.

"A woman just hit her child." She pointed to the deli. "I think the baby can't breathe."

The guard spoke into his walkie-talkie, and Julie entered the library.

Derek had insisted on carpet, an oatmeal shag, for the top floor, where they had their bedrooms.

The threads caught on Angela's heels. Her family had had a cat when she was young, a short-haired scrawny black thing named Opi. They were always forgetting to clip its nails. The cat had walked slowly around their bungalow, lifting each limb to unhook its claws one paw at a time.

He was lying on the bed with a cold compress on his eyes, his feet on the pillows.

"You can't leave me out there alone. I look like shit."

A glass of Scotch sat on the bedside table. Usually he drank it on the rocks.

He'd started making money, real money, four years into their marriage, when Teya was just a baby. Neither came from it, but Derek took to it easily, reserving tables at the newest restaurants, ordering bottles of expensive wine, $100, $200, sometimes more. He bought her a Chanel purse and thousand-dollar riding boots. She tucked the purse into the back of her closet, it had a giant logo on the front, and wore the boots in all weather so that salt crept up the sides and stained the brown leather a crusty grey.

"Is there an emergency?"

With his eyes covered, his chin upside down, his face looked like a talking potato. As children, she and her sister drew eyes on their chins, held tea towels over their noses and eyes, and talked and laughed and laughed.

"No."

"Then fuck off."

Julie passed Loupa in the hallway. The girl was prettier than any of them had been at twenty-two, her nose coming to a delicate point, her cheeks high and flushed, her mouth a pout. She was Polish.

"How's the princess?"

"Asleep, finally." Loupa smiled and rolled her eyes.

"Have a drink."

"Maybe," she said.

George had started building the crib in secret the moment Julie announced her intentions. He had soundproofed the basement and set up a woodworking space when they bought the place. The thwack of hammers and whir of the grinders bled up through the ceiling. He always had a project going: teak jewellery boxes, a chestnut coffee table, a set of cherry dining room chairs.

They visited a doctor after six months and were told to come back after a year; she was under thirty-five. She told them about the cyst she'd had removed at eighteen, a little orb on her left ovary filled with hair and bone and skin; it ached every month and made her feel full all the time. But no, that wouldn't have had an effect.

They ruled out George and then examined her.

The doctor's office had a low ceiling and was dark; they were in an old wing of the hospital.

"Your eggs are still viable," he said. He placed one hand on top of the other. "But your fallopian tubes are blocked." Beneath his hands he revealed a picture of her uterus.

"Here and here," he said.

The scans were blotchy, a Rorschach, her womb.

The girls had taken a trip to Europe after

graduation; all three, even though Julie thought it would be easier to travel just two.

She had planned the itinerary. They landed in London, stumbled about the city jet-lagged, and then ferried to Amsterdam.

Angela bought a couple pre-rolled joints in a café, even though Maryanne said she could roll just fine.

"It's less messy," Angela said, and they smoked the first joint.

On the street, they each bought a cone of french fries, drizzled with mayonnaise.

"This is the best thing I have ever eaten," Maryanne said, and Angela and Julie nodded.

In the red-light district, girls wearing lingerie sat in lit windows. One, her long bleached hair coiled on top of her head in braids, reclined on her chair and talked on a cellphone.

"They put the pretty ones out front," Maryanne said. "But you actually get an uglier one in the back."

"How would you know?" Julie asked.

"My brother came last year," she said.

They walked to the Heineken Museum and got the package tour, which included a special edition pint glass in a decorative green tin and a drink at the end. The bartender poured them one after another. They sat in a group of boys from Australia and America and drank until the bar shut down. Then they moved to a beer garden where Angela lit the other joint and passed it around. When it was really late, the girls couldn't remember how to get to the hostel, so they went with the boys. Julie liked an Australian named Myles, a tall boy with crooked teeth, but Angela took him by the arm. Maryanne had hit it off with another Australian at the museum bar. On the way, an American squeezed Julie's ribs, and she squealed from surprise and because it tickled, and it was settled.

The next day, Julie had a sore back. The boys all shared a dorm room, but they had their own bunks.

They ate crepes on the street and found the hostel with no problem; it was close to the museum.

"I think you guys did it on the stairway," Maryanne said. She'd gotten the Australian's email. "Don't you remember?"

The guests had started dancing; someone had turned up the stereo and changed the music, a throbbing bass.

Pierre was still smoking on the terrace.

"Can I have one?" Angela asked.

Skinny snowflakes fell though the sky was clear.

He handed her his cigarette and she took a drag. The filter was hot in her mouth; he was an aggressive smoker.

"I want my own," she said. He rattled the pack and slid one out for her.

George opened the door to the terrace. His glass of wine, half full, was smudged with fingerprints.

"I didn't know you smoked," he said. "Can I have another?" he asked Pierre. "I totally owe you."

"I used to smoke all the time," Angela said.

No one had changed the ashtrays and a few butts had spilled out onto the floor. Angela nudged them over the side of the terrace with her shoe.

"When you were an actress?" Pierre asked.

"Did you know Pierre is a poet?" George said.

"I had no idea."

"He's going to Toronto in the fall. What kind of program is it?"

"An MFA," Pierre said, and looked at the cigarette in his hand.

"Holy shit, Angela, what happened to your eye?" George said.

"Oh, I'm such a klutz," she said. She crossed her arms and took a drag. The cigarette tasted like nothing.

A couple nights before, Angela had bought three tests. She lined the sticks up on the counter next to the drop-down sink, a sunken rectangle of stone. The entire bathroom was a soft green marble. Angela had scrubbed the counter with baking soda and vinegar when they first moved in, and the sheen had dulled. Still, she wouldn't allow the cleaner in. Toothpaste, soap, her blonde hairs, Derek's bristle crusted the bottom of the sink; it never drained properly.

Probably she left a test wrapper on the counter. She spent the evening throwing up in the hall bathroom, snuck in a kiss to Teya, said good night. Loupa was such a sport.

That night after Teya was asleep and Loupa had gone out and they were alone, he asked her, "What are you about?" He was sitting on his side on top of the covers, reading. He looked up at her over his wire glasses.

She was already in her nightie, a gauzy blue

chemise thing; they hadn't slept together in almost a year.

He pulled the wrapper out from the book, as though it were a marker.

"What the hell is this?"

He had given her a black eye when she was in college, but they had just been play fighting. She had bit his forearm and then shadowboxed him, and he shadowboxed back but clipped her eye. It had been a small bruise, a blue crescent swelling under her right eye.

She ran to the bathroom not because she was afraid but because of the nausea. She tripped and fell, that carpet was everywhere, her right arm cocked just so that her eye landed squarely on her fist.

"I'm such a klutz," Angela repeated.

"Did I tell you about my first passion?" George was asking Pierre. "Woodwork. I could have apprenticed with a real master." He shook his head.

Julie walked up the circular staircase to the second floor, where she was eye level with the top of the tree and the vintage angel, eyes cast upwards, its flaking face framed in yellowing lace. On the third level, where they slept, the carpet sucked up the click of her heels.

The doctor had cited a number of possible causes: endometriosis, post-surgery complications, STIs. He explained that some asymptomatic STIs, if left untreated, scarred up the tubes, creating blockage.

Julie had seen the cradle, in a corner of the workroom, by accident. She never went in there, everything was sharp, but had to ask about the taxes, and George had his back turned; the grinder made a racket.

He'd carved little moons in the cherry all the way around the top of the cradle, above the spindles.

Of course they had other options, the doctor had explained. Surgery, in-vitro, adoption. Foreign adoption was very popular, and faster.

Angela had chosen flying sheep and clouds against a green pastoral, a neutral because she had wanted a surprise. The child slept with curled fists and an open mouth, her face damp, a tooth missing between parted lips. She had Angela's hair, but maybe she would need to dye it later on; Derek was darker.

The party thrummed downstairs, trills of

laughter, the deep drum of the stereo.

George had dismantled the cradle and repurposed the wood. That Christmas, he gave her a wooden heart on a gold chain. She never wore it.

Next to Teya's bed sat a little box made of cherry, a peephole in the top carved like a moon. Julie picked it up; knick-knacks rattled and a little bell pinged. She opened the box: a red velvet cat collar, a plastic wind-up duck from the inside of a European chocolate egg, a little stone, just a regular piece of gravel, all rested inside. The child turned her head and expelled breath like in a sigh.

The day before, in the morning before lunch at the deli, Julie had received a phone call from the agency; one government was tightening regulations and the other didn't care. The adoption was a no go. Far below her office, the highway shone black, snow was falling, and the river steamed. She rode the elevator down ten stories to the mezzanine. Birds flew among the deciduous trees. The space reminded Julie of a hollowed pyramid, which perhaps had been the point. The architect was famous, but she couldn't remember his name.

Angela and Derek had four bedrooms upstairs, but they only used two. The master was at the end of the long, skinny hallway, with an en suite and a massive walk-in, rows of pegs along one wall for Angela's shoes. She had shown Julie and said, "How can I ever fill these?" but she had. The door was ajar and Julie pushed the mahogany and it swung open easily.

Derek sat on the bed, reading, and drinking from a tumbler, a bottle, half full of brown liquid, next to him.

"Not social tonight?"

"Did Angela send you?"

He set his glass down on the bedside table that was tall and built into the wall, custom-made.

"Did you give her the shiner?"

The bed was king size and covered in burgundy velvet. All the pillows, a deep navy and also velvet, were piled on the other side of the bed.

"Want a drink?"

He kept glasses in the bedside table and poured a two fingers' width of liquid into a glass and gave it to her. She sat on the edge of the bed next to him.

"Did you choose the duvet?"

"Probably the designer," he said, fingers skimming his forehead.

"Does it ever get embarrassing? The money."

She drank, it was Scotch, and her throat burned.

"That's rude," he said, and paused. "Sometimes it's uncomfortable."

His lips shone pale pink next to his black stubble. Julie began to perspire; she felt both cool and flushed.

He lifted a hand and stroked the back of her sweater.

"Don't you find this itchy?"

In the kitchen, someone had arranged the pieces of the broken fruit bowl and piled the pots and pans on the side counter, but the bananas were gone. Sève and the servers were cleaning.

"Is it midnight already?" Angela asked, and poured a glass of water and another of wine.

They had a system: one server washed a glass, another dried it, a third placed it into its tray. Like a cottage industry, Angela thought.

She topped up her glass and walked to the hallway.

The dancing guests waved their arms and flung their hips to the left and right, just as they had every year, although when everyone smoked pot, there was less dancing. The candles around the wall burned still, ridges of wax had floated over their sides and pooled on the hardwood.

Maryanne separated from the crowd. She was holding the underside of her belly.

"I've been trying to dance this baby out," Maryanne said. Her mascara had slid into the creases around her eyes.

"I'm surprised you made it this far." They kissed each other on the cheeks, air kisses without touching each other.

"To be young again," Maryanne said.

"Did Mireille take your coat? It must be in the foyer." They walked to the entrance, where Mireille had hung the coat. "Text me when it comes," Angela said.

Maryanne left in a cab, and the snow came harder; the sky had greyed behind the falling white.

Angela walked back into the party and wondered when everyone would leave; her face had started to throb again, the painkillers worn off and the wine causing its own headache. Just on the outskirts of the throng, a pop like a gunshot exploded, and a spray of glass, little chunks, hit Angela's thigh. A candle had tipped in its holder, and the heat proved too much for the glass, which was shaped like a palm, a regular decoration she kept year-round.

A dancer, one of Derek's techie friends,

jumped up and back into the tree. The man swayed forward, and the tree as well, forward and back. Then it teetered to the side and crashed, blocking the entrance to the terrace.

The dancers screamed, and the decorations, all the antique Christmas balls, the hand-painted ceramic bird ornaments, the Austrian crystal orbs, smashed. A crimson ball rolled towards Angela. Even after the renovations, the floors still slanted.

A flame licked up the wall.

When Derek petted her back, Julie shrugged her shoulders up to her ears from the prickling pain.

"It hurts," Julie said.

"Lift your arms."

She set the glass down and lifted them up like a child. Derek pulled the sweater over her head; the collar got stuck at her chin, and he yanked it up. She sucked in her stomach.

"Turn over," he said, and she lay on the bed. "Your skin is red."

He pressed a cool palm to her skin, then set the glasses of Scotch on her and then removed them.

"Feel better?" He started rubbing above the

band of her tights, sunk his thumbs into the dimples in her lower back. "It's tense here," he said, and kept massaging until he lifted her hips up and slid her tights down over her hips to her knees.

He massaged the backs of her thighs but she pushed his head away when he kissed them. He lifted her up by the hips and she rose to all fours. Her hands and knees sank into the duvet; it was down and plush.

He unzipped and shifted his weight. She could feel him kneeling behind her, and then he pressed himself into her. The bed was too large to register their rocking.

The sound like a gunshot stopped their breath. They looked to the door. Derek had braced himself against Julie's hips, but now his fingers reached around and touched the pouch of her belly.

The door opened, and the child, face puffy with sleep, called for her mother, and then her eyes grew large.

Julie dove away from him and rolled off the bed, and Derek covered himself and said, "Baby, baby, wait."

The flames crawled up the wall and through the tree, which was synthetic because Angela hadn't wanted needles everywhere, although now the branches were melting. Angela tasted the plastic burn in her mouth.

"Call 911," she said, but the guests had backed up away from the fire, huddling in the foyer, streaming out the door.

George pounded on the sliding door glass; smoke rose and obscured his figure.

Sève, thank god for Sève, appeared with the extinguisher and sprayed foam, flecks landing on the trilling sparks, dousing them. A chemical smell, sweet and sticky, filled the room.

Loupa ran up the stairs, and Teya, out of bed of course, ran to her and they embraced. On the terrace, George was alone now. Pierre must have jumped the railing; he could climb down using the fire escape, that's what it was for.

Angela's stomach cramped, probably from the wine, but she imagined the little clump of cells wiggling away, fighting like mad to get out. She had booked the appointment for Monday; it didn't have long to stay.

Derek was on the stairs, taking Teya from Loupa, and then Julie, dear Julie, came after him.

"I don't blame you," she said, holding her stomach. "I don't blame you one bit."

Going to Market

Pastor Mike said to come on the Saturday; Sunday he'd be busy.

"Perfect," Maya said. Weekends they went to the market; she and Fynn had driven past the church every Saturday that summer. They bought grass-fed beef and heirloom tomatoes, sometimes a dozen farm eggs, brown feathers still stuck to the tanned and spackled shells. They used to go to the market in town, but then it moved locations; now it had a food court, and there was never any parking. So Maya and Fynn drove from the north side of the river through downtown, across the suburbs, and into the foothills on the secondary highway that had no lanes. They passed spandexed cyclists, torsos bent parallel to the road, legs ninety degree pistons, pumping. They rolled up the windows when they passed the fields of stinking yellow flowers. The church looked like an old school house and sat in front of two green rolling hills, as though a child had sketched it into the landscape.

Today they skipped brunch and left the house early; Maya packed the cloth sacks and the cooler for the meat, and Fynn brought the coffee, black, for both.

"Is there snow on the mountains?" Maya asked as they turned west towards the church.

"That's just the sun reflecting," Fynn said. He chewed his lip; he had once confessed, early on, that he used to chain-smoke on road trips. But that was a long time ago.

The sun glinted off the church's white clapboard. A modest wooden cross sat on top of the steepled roof. Gravel pinged off their hatchback's tires as Fynn drove around the circular lot and then parked the car. It was already hot and a swarm of mosquitos hung next to Maya's window. She shooed them away as she got out.

"Close your door, quick," Maya said. Her cork wedge heels sunk into the gravel. "Remember to take pictures," she said.

The church was small, but they wanted no

more than eighty guests. They would set up a tent out back and rent a barbeque, serve corn and a dessert of apple, which would be in season, perhaps as a crisp. They didn't want a cake.

When they had met with the wedding planner, Maya said she wanted a country vibe: checkered flags in muted primary colours, candles in mason jars, a bouquet of actual wildflowers, lots of little strings of lights hung between the trees and in the tent, a photo booth in the back for the guests, with props like empty picture frames and feather boas.

"Something simple," Fynn had said. The planner talked them out of balloons.

Each week after the market, they always picnicked at a park called Red Deer Lake, though the lake was more of a slough. Someone had let the grass grow up around the picnic tables and over the tops of the rusting garbage bins. But the birds came because of the water, and Maya and Fynn sat cross-legged on top of their favourite picnic table overlooking the water, the mountains behind them. They snacked on beef jerky and salted tomato halves. The day Fynn proposed, he sliced the tomatoes and stuck the ring, a ruby solitaire in yellow gold, into Maya's half.

Fynn knocked on the double doors and then

tried the latch, but it was locked. Beige paint flaked off the handle.

"Around here," Pastor Mike called from the side of the church. They followed him around the corner and entered into a kitchen covered in green linoleum. The tiles were scuffed, their edges curling upwards. Pastor Mike flicked switches, but no lights came on.

"I don't spend a lot of time in here," he said.

"We can use the kitchen?" Maya asked. The fridge had only one door and was a pale yellow.

"You guys want to get married, is that right?"

Pastor Mike walked from the kitchen into the sanctuary, which had been carpeted in navy blue. Between the rows of wooden pews, the floor had turned a shade of pale denim. Light pierced the stained glass behind the black cross and dappled the altar in white spots. It smelled of drying wool.

"We could put a runner here," Maya said, pointing to the aisle. "Fynn, take a picture."

He took a picture with his phone. Maya stood in one spot, turning. Wood panels reached up the walls all the way around.

"I didn't have time to change," Pastor Mike said. He wore jeans ripped at the left thigh, black staining both knees. "It's harvest."

"Oh, we love the market," Maya said.

"The market?" Pastor Mike sucked in air between his back teeth. His left canine was the colour of lead. "I don't know anything about that. We do alfalfa and rapeseed."

"Oh," Maya said. She rubbed at her collarbone with her thumb.

"You'd know it as canola." He swished his tongue around his mouth behind closed lips.

"Does September work?" Fynn asked. He took a photo of the entrance to the bathrooms, *Ladies* and *Gentlemen* spelled out in cursive wooden letters above each door. "Next September, I mean."

"Why you documenting the toilets?" A smell of oil and something sweet came off the Pastor.

"Just for the planner, to give her an idea of the space."

"Fancy," Pastor Mike said.

"Fynn, come take a picture of this," Maya said. She walked to the front of the church.

They wanted an acreage one day, or at least a cabin, or what Fynn called a cottage; he was from out east. A few chickens, a garden definitely, wildflowers, maybe a goat. Now they were inner city, living in a 1912 bungalow, a rental. But it was one or the other, downtown or the country, nothing in between.

"I grew up thinking lettuce came out of cardboard boxes wrapped in plastic," Maya had said on an early date. She had grown up in a pastel suburb in a baby blue split-level. Her mother had tried to grow tomatoes in the backyard but planted them in the shade; she had once killed a cactus.

"Will the wood work?" Maya said to Fynn when he reached her close to the altar. She scratched at a mole on her neck. She lowered her voice and said, "I thought it was different from the road."

"Rain's coming," Pastor Mike said. He was right behind them. "Damn mosquitos will have a heyday."

"The sky is clear," Maya said.

Pastor Mike scratched at a fresh bite on his forehead. His fingernails were black-ringed. He tapped his nose.

"I can smell it," he said.

Maya sniffed; all she smelled was the floor of the church and the Pastor. His odour had ripened, like that of a browning banana.

"So you two are part of the church, then?" Pastor Mike folded his arms across his chest. His shirt was white with faint stains, faded brown splashes along the collar.

"We're not really religious, honestly," Maya said.

"But we've been baptized, yes," Fynn said. He

was still taking photos: detail shots, close-ups of the pews, the black nails that screwed them into the floor.

"You sure do like that phone of yours," Pastor Mike said to Fynn. "We do counselling; it's mandatory." He rocked back on his heels. A skittering noise came from the roof. "Those are the birds."

"It sounds like someone's throwing pebbles," Maya said.

The experts advised she secure a venue first, but Maya had already tried on dresses. The one she liked was a creamy A-line, just covering her toes, with ribbons criss-crossing up the back; sophisticated but, she thought, a bit vintage, a bit country. The shots of her and Fynn, in a brown suit, she already had one in mind, outside would be charming. But inside, the wood, a classroom brown, would be in every shot.

"You two live together, then?" Pastor Mike sucked back air again like he was trying to loosen seeds from his molars.

"Does that make a difference?" Fynn asked.

"So you do, then." Pastor Mike's upper lip covered his teeth when he smiled. "Of course it does. We do different counselling."

"We?" Maya said. She wanted earthy tones—

they would be getting married in the fall. Perhaps a burnt orange.

"My wife, Susan," Pastor Mike said. "The feminine touch."

A guttural rumble, like a groan, started out past the church, deep in the ground.

"There she comes," Pastor Mike said.

"Your wife?" Maya said.

The rain arrived as soft thuds on the roof, and the church dimmed as though someone had thrown a sheet over it.

"The car," Maya said. "The sunroof."

Fynn walked to the entrance, tried the double doors, one and then the other, but they were locked.

"Open the doors," he said. He shook the handles and the doors rattled.

"It won't do you any good," Pastor Mike said. He pulled out a key from his pocket and unlocked the doors. Fynn pushed the Pastor aside.

A waterfall burst from the sky in front of him.

Fynn backed away from the door. He wiped the water splatter on his glasses with his shirt.

A crack of lightning hit the steps outside the door and sizzled the water.

The water soaked the ground and floated the

gravel, it dropped from leaks in the roof to the floor all along the aisle. It reached up the steps and tongued the entrance of the church, spilled over the threshold and into the sanctuary, darkened the carpets and then soaked them.

Maya pointed to the car, a blurry white behind the currents; the water moved it gently up and around, twirling it slowly in place.

The water was to their knees. They followed Pastor Mike away from the door, climbed onto the front pew, then waded to the altar.

The Pastor hummed a marching tune and climbed up the cross, weightless. The water was above Maya's head, and they swam to the cross and pulled themselves higher; rust had pimpled the black paint. They hung to the tip until the water reached three feet from the pointed roof. Fynn and the Pastor kicked out the stained glass; it was fragile. Maya slit the side of her hand swimming out, and the red spread around her to a pale pink before it stopped. The water was cold.

The roof was tacky and still hot, the car long gone.

"Do something," Fynn said to Pastor Mike.

"The harvest is ruined," Pastor Mike said.

Water, still rising, shimmered to the mountains, but the rain had stopped.

Acknowledgements

So many people have helped, directly and indirectly, in the writing of this book; more than I can mention here, and I am grateful to them all. To Jon Paul Fiorentino, for believing in this project; to my teachers, Aritha van Herk, Mikhail Iossel, and Mary di Michele, for guidance, mentorship, and expertise; to my fellow students in all the creative writing classes I have taken at the University of Calgary and Concordia University, for critiques and comradery; to Sarah Selecky, the Banff Centre, and the Little Stones, especially Paige Cooper, Frances Phillips, Kristyn Dunnion, and Phoebe Tsang, for lighting a fire and then helping me sustain it; to the Natalie Simpson Writers Group for the Illiterate and Visually Impaired, for community and Sunday afternoon inspiration; to Sarah Ftichar, Sara Leishman, Katie Lewandowski, Adam Carlson, Sachiko Murakami, Johanna Skibsrud, and Dan Pinese, for friendship; to my parents, for so much love and support; and to my partner and reader, Colin, for everything and love—thank you.

Jani Krulc lives in Calgary with her partner and their animals, Pinot and Gigi.